JASON STRANGE

Realm of Ghosts

Cover Illustration by Serg Soleiman

Interior Illustration by Phil Parks

STONE ARCH BOOKS
a capstone imprint

Jason Strange is published by Stone Arch Books
A Capstone Imprint
1710 Roe Crest Drive
North Mankato, Minnesota 56003
www.capstonepub.com

Copyright © 2011 by Stone Arch Books

Library of Congress Cataloging-in-Publication Data is available on
the Library of Congress website.

Library Binding: 978-1-4342-2962-5
Paperback: 978-1-4342-3096-6

Summary: Does a battle online mean death IRL?

Art Director/Graphic Designer: Kay Fraser
Production Specialist: Michelle Biedscheid

Photo credits:
Shutterstock: Nikita Rogul (handcuffs, p. 2); Stephen Mulcahey (police badge, p. 2);
B&T Media Group (blank badge, p. 2); Picsfive (coffee stain, pp. 2, 5, 14, 25, 34, 40,
49, 58); Andy Dean Photography (paper, pen, coffee, pp. 2, 66); osov (blank notes,
p. 1); Thomas M Perkins (folder with blank paper, pp. 64, 65); M.E. Mulder (black
electrical tape, pp. 67, 68, 69)

Printed in the United States of America.
071318   000756

TABLE OF CONTENTS

– Chapter 1: **Kingdom of Doom** –

Curtis Switzer leaned over his computer keyboard and mouse. He moved the mouse at lightning speed. With his left hand, he pounded away at the number keys along the top of the keyboard.

He knew that anyone watching wouldn't have found it very exciting, but on the computer screen, it was a violent battle to the death.

Curtis was playing *Kingdom of Doom*. His friend Tom Yackish, Jr., who everyone just called Junior, was standing next to him.

"Curtis," Junior said.

Curtis barely heard him. In the game, Curtis was controlling his favorite avatar, Hurricane, a warrior. His opponent was a very crafty thief called King.

"Curtis," Junior said again. This time Curtis felt his friend's finger poke into his shoulder.

"Quit it," Curtis said. "I'm about to finish off this thief."

The thief, King, was a tough opponent. That was unusual for Curtis. Usually he downed other players easily.

In fact, Hurricane was sort of famous as the best fighter in the realm.

"This guy's good," Curtis said. "I've never played against him before. Never heard of him, even."

"I don't know how you can play this game," Junior said. He moved to the bed and lay down, tossing a basketball up a few feet and catching it again. He wasn't as into video games as Curtis. Then again, no one ever was.

"I mean, you don't even know that guy," Junior went on. "How can you get into this intense death match with some random guy over the Internet?"

"Huh?" Curtis replied. He wasn't paying attention. He glanced at the thief's health meter. A few more good hits and Curtis would be the winner — Hurricane would be victorious again.

Suddenly, the thief puffed in a cloud of smoke. Before Curtis knew it, King the thief had appeared behind him. He tried to spin Hurricane around quickly to stop the attack, but King was too fast.

Hurricane was down.

"No way," Curtis muttered. He leaned back in his chair and watched King the thief dance around Hurricane's fallen body. "He beat me."

"Oh, I'm so sorry," Junior said, rolling his eyes. He got up from the bed. "Can we move on to pressing matters?"

"You don't understand," Curtis said. He spun around in his fancy gaming chair so that he was facing Junior. "Hurricane has never lost a duel before. He's the best player in the realm!"

"You mean you're the best player in the realm," Junior said. "Hurricane isn't a real guy, dude."

"You know what I mean," Curtis said. He spun back to his desk. Quickly, he logged off of the game and switched off his monitor. "This is a total bummer."

"Agreed," Junior said, getting up and pacing the room. "Now, let's move on to this party we've been invited to."

"Oh, not this again," Curtis said with a groan. He got up from his chair and lay on the bed.

He grabbed a gaming magazine from his nightstand and started flipping through it. Curtis skimmed quickly through an article on a champion gamer named Khyber Kingsley.

"Did you hear about this guy, Khyber Kingsley?" he asked Junior. "He was profiled in *Gamer* last month, and now he's missing. He's been missing for a week or so, I guess."

"Quit changing the subject," Junior said. "And no, I've never heard of that guy. Come on, let's go to the party."

"You know how I feel about that party," Curtis said, turning a page in his magazine.

"Come on!" Junior pleaded. "Have a change of heart, for my sake. We're talking about a party thrown by Troy Macintosh. He invited me personally — left a message on my cell phone this morning. All of the coolest kids in school are going to be there. Do you know what this could mean for us? If we go to this party tonight, we could become popular."

"What do I care about popularity?" Curtis said. He flipped to the "New Games" section of his magazine. "If you're popular, people just pay more attention to you. Who wants that?"

"I do!" Junior said, pointing at his chest. "Me! I want more attention!"

"Not me. I'm fine just sitting in my room and gaming," Curtis said. "That's good enough for me."

Junior grabbed Curtis by the shoulders and stared into his eyes. "Please," he said. "Do this for me and I will never ask another favor of you."

Curtis rolled his eyes. "Fine," he said. "For you, I'll go, but I won't enjoy myself."

"Of course you will," Junior said, smiling. "It's at DigiGame."

"What?!" Curtis said. He sat up straight and threw the magazine down onto the already-messy floor. "Why didn't you tell me it was at DigiGame? That's the best gaming club in town."

Junior shrugged. "I didn't think you'd want anyone to see you gaming," he admitted. "You know, in the spotlight and everything."

Curtis sagged. Junior was right. If they went to that party and Curtis played as well as he usually did, everyone would know he was great at something. He didn't want the attention. Worse still, everyone would find out he was Hurricane the warrior, the best player in the realm.

That wasn't a secret Curtis was looking forward to getting out.

But a promise was a promise. "All right,"
he said, standing up. "Let's get out of here.
But I'm warning you, if this party is lame,
I'm out of there."

– Chapter 2: **DigiGame** –

It was a warm night, so the boys decided to walk across town to the warehouse district.

"Maybe this is a bad idea," Curtis said. "Like you were saying."

"Um, I never said this was a bad idea," Junior replied.

"Sure you did," Curtis said. "You pointed out that for me, this party at DigiGame might be a bad idea."

"Whatever," Junior said. "We're almost there anyway. Just relax. If you want, pretend to play badly. Create a new avatar. A wizard or something. No one has to know you're Hurricane, I promise."

"I guess that could work," Curtis said. "It wouldn't be the worst thing to have a new avatar to mess around with."

The two boys turned onto Water Street. DigiGame was at the end of the block on the dead-end street, just before the retaining wall and the river. But even from the corner, they could tell something wasn't right at the big brick building.

"The lights are off at DigiGame," Curtis said. He stopped under a flickering streetlight. "It looks abandoned or something. Did they close down?"

"Impossible," Junior said. He grabbed Curtis's arm to pull him along. "Troy wouldn't plan a party at DigiGame if DigiGame was closed. Think about it, Curtis. Duh."

Curtis groaned, but he started walking again. Not a single light was on at DigiGame's end of the block. All of the windows were dark.

"This doesn't look safe," Curtis said. "We should head back."

"Come on. It's fine," Junior insisted. He started walking faster. "Let's just hurry up and get inside."

But when Curtis and Junior got closer to the building, they saw that there was no way inside. The front door and the windows were boarded up with planks of wood.

"Told you," Curtis said, shaking his head. "This place is closed. Let's get out of here." He turned to leave.

"Wait a second," Junior said. "There's a piece of paper on the ground. It looks like it was ripped off the door."

Curtis sighed loudly, but he followed as Junior went to check out the paper.

"Closed until further notice," Junior read out loud, "due to an electrical accident last week. Sorry for the inconvenience."

"There you go," Curtis said. "It's closed. Now can we go home?"

"No way," Junior said. "Why would Troy have a party here if the place was closed?"

Curtis shook his head. "I don't know," he said. Then it came to him. He slapped himself in the forehead.

"It was a trick," he said. "That's all it was. Troy and his popular friends played a little trick on us."

"You're crazy," Junior said. He was busy trying to peer through the wood boards into the club. Curtis followed him as he made his way around the side of the building.

"Am I?" Curtis said. "We're the only ones here, the place is closed, and obviously there is no party going on. I bet they're getting us on video right now. It'll be all over the Internet by Monday morning."

"Give me a boost, will you?" Junior asked. He was trying to look in a window on the side of the building.

"You're wasting your time," Curtis said, but he put out his hands so that Junior could jump up.

"Aha!" Junior said. He was at eye level with a little crack in the wood over the window. "I see some lights in there."

"Really?" Curtis asked. "Are you sure?"

"Yup," Junior replied. "And there are some shadows, like someone's moving around." He jumped down.

"Probably a burglar," Curtis said. "Or a homeless person, looking for somewhere to sleep."

"Let's try the front door," Junior said. He hurried around to the front of the building.

"It's boarded up," Curtis said, jogging after his friend. "Remember?"

Still, Junior ran to the front door. He knocked on the board, thumping his fist hard.

"This is so dumb," Curtis said. He leaned against the door, and to his surprise, it swung right open.

Curtis fell into the club, right onto the black-and-white tile floor. He looked up at Junior.

"You were saying?" Junior said, smiling. He put out his hand to help. Curtis grabbed it and pulled himself to his feet.

The boys looked around. The place was very dark and quiet. A faint sound — almost like a humming — came from a room around the corner.

"The computers must be that way," Junior said. He started around the corner.

"This doesn't really feel like a party to me," Curtis said, trailing behind. "There's no one here."

When they entered the computer room, he knew he was right. The room, though full of computers, was empty of people.

All the computers were off and covered in dust. The ceiling had most of its tiles removed, and Curtis could see the wiring, still under repair.

"Let's look in the other rooms," Junior said.

Curtis sighed. "Whatever," he said.

A single light flickered in the corridor. Curtis kept his hand on the wall as he moved slowly through the club.

There were overturned chairs here and there. Several had been broken, and one looked like it had been in a fire. It was blackened, and one of its legs had broken off.

"I don't like this, Junior," Curtis said. "Let's just get out of here, okay? Come on. None of the computers are even on. There's no point."

"This one's on," Junior said. He was crouched over a computer in the farthest corner of the room, close to a door marked OFFICE. "The screen's blank, though," he added.

Curtis went over to join him. "The screen saver came on, that's all," he said, grabbing the mouse. "Here."

When Curtis moved the mouse, the screen clicked and flashed into life — barely. The display popped and shook, and the glowing screen flickered on and off.

"Something's coming up," Junior said. They leaned closer.

The screen glowed red, and letters began to form in black, like thousands of flies landing to form words.

Curtis stared as the sentence became clear. "If you can read this, it's already too late."

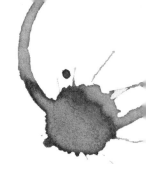

– Chapter 3: **Too Late** –

Curtis grabbed Junior's wrist. "We're going," he said. "Now."

Junior nodded. "Yeah," he said. "This place got real weird real fast."

The two boys moved quickly through the computer room. The placement of tables made it hard to move quickly. Cables ran along the floor, tripping them up and slowing them down.

Computers whirred to life as they passed, and displays popped and fizzed on and off. Curtis caught glimpses of the screens as he and Junior pushed through the room.

Games started and began playing on their own. Explosions rang out. The blood-curdling screams of game characters and the crazed laughter of villains rang through the room.

One monitor showed a new message. "Too late."

Another showed a skull, rocking back and forth with laughter.

On another, a thief from *Kingdom of Doom* waved his dagger at Curtis — or it seemed like he was waving the long knife at Curtis, anyway.

Finally, the boys reached the hallway.

"This is some practical joke," Junior said.

"We have to tell someone," Curtis said. "Troy can't get away with this. It has to be totally illegal."

The front door was still standing open. But just as the boys reached it, the flickering overhead bulb shattered with a loud pop and the door slammed closed.

Curtis and Junior stopped and stared at the door.

"Um," Curtis said, "let me see that invite Troy gave you."

Junior shook his head. "He left me a voice mail," he said, pulling out his cell phone. "There's no service in here, though, or I'd play it for you."

"Great," Curtis said. "I'm officially scared now."

Junior banged on the door. "Hello?" he called out. "Anyone out there?"

"Troy?" Curtis shouted. "Very funny. You win. Can we go now?"

Silence.

"Okay, there has to be another way out, right?" Curtis said. "For emergencies."

Junior looked around. "I don't see one," he said. "The only other door I even saw was to the office, in the computer room."

Curtis nodded. "Right, I saw it, too," he said. "I'm not so sure I want to go back that way, though. This place totally freaks me out. It's haunted or something."

"Come on," Junior said, rolling his eyes. "It's just a practical joke that Troy's playing on us. He may not be the computer whiz you are, but I'm sure he could manage this."

Curtis thought about it. Most of what had happened could be explained with some simple programming and rewiring. "I suppose you're right," he agreed. "Let's go."

Junior opened his cell phone. He had no service, so he knew he couldn't call for help, but the phone still lit up when he opened it. The light shined down the corridor. "Come on," he said. "Follow me."

Curtis followed behind his friend. Junior's cell phone lit the computer room with its eerie blue light. The flickering shadows of the monitors cast some light, too. As Curtis and Junior walked toward the corner office, the cackles and screams from the games, still running on the computers, broke the silence.

"Troy must be good," Curtis said quietly, almost in a whisper. "Some of these computers aren't even connected to a server."

"Huh," Junior said.

"That one isn't even plugged in," Curtis added, nodding toward the biggest computer, near the window. The cord had been cut. "But it's running *Kingdom of Doom*."

They stood in front of the office door.

"Think it's open?" Junior asked.

"Might as well try it," Curtis said. He grabbed the knob. It turned, and Curtis swung the door open.

The office was a mostly empty room. It was almost completely dark. The only light was the dim glow of a computer monitor sitting in the middle of a metal table.

On the far side of the room was a big metal door. A red sign across it read "Emergency Exit Only."

"Let's go," Junior said, and he started through the door.

As Curtis followed, though, the monitor on the desk flashed brightly. Both boys stopped and covered their eyes. They'd grown used to the dark by now, so the flash hurt their eyes. The sound of a video game explosion burst in their ears.

Curtis reached for the monitor, trying to turn it off. As he stuck out his hand, it went suddenly black.

Junior and Curtis looked at the screen. Soon red letters appeared, like drops of liquid rolling together. They began to form into words. As Curtis read them, he heard a voice from behind him, speaking the same words that had appeared on the screen. "I told you, there is no escape."

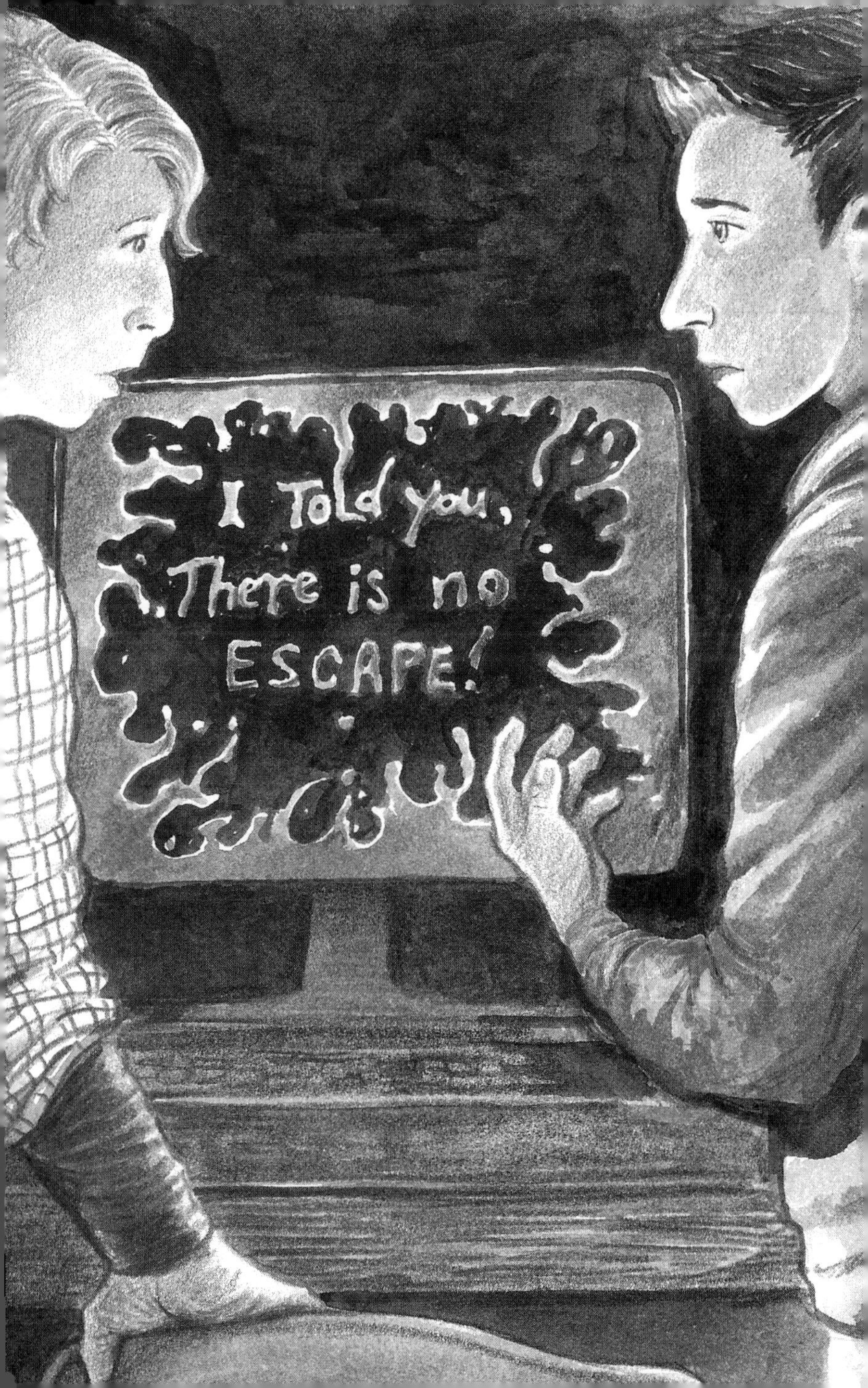
I Told you,
There is no
ESCAPE!

– Chapter 4: **Challenge** –

Curtis and Junior spun around. There, in the doorway of the office, was a tall figure. He wore all black, even a black hood that hung low, so the shadow covered his face.

"Who — who are you?" Junior asked, backing away.

Curtis backed up until his back was against the metal table in the middle of the room. The speakers on the monitor behind him laughed and cackled.

"Just don't hurt us," Curtis said.

The figure didn't move toward them. He just stood in the doorway, staring.

"Is — is that you, Troy?" Junior said, trying to laugh. "Okay, very funny. Joke over, okay? You win. You got us."

The figure remained silent. Behind the boys, the monitor flashed and cast their shadows against the wall.

"Um, hello?" Junior said. "Creepy guy?"

The figure raised his hand to silence Junior. As he did, the laughter coming out of the monitor behind them stopped, too. The figure reached up and removed his hood, revealing his face.

It wasn't Troy. The man's face was thin and pale, and his eyes looked sunken, like he hadn't slept in weeks.

His dark hair was shaggy and fell past his ears. His eyes, slate gray, seemed to glow in the poorly lit room.

For some reason, Curtis felt like he recognized him.

"You will not leave this club," the man said, staring at Curtis. "You will not leave until you have accepted my challenge."

"What challenge?" Junior said.

The man slowly turned his head and faced Junior. "You are of no concern to me, noob," he said. "My challenge is for Hurricane."

"Hurricane?" Junior repeated. "Who's Hurricane?"

Curtis looked at Junior.

"Oh, yeah," Junior said quietly. "You are."

Curtis looked at the man in black. "How do you know who I am?" he asked.

The man smiled, and his lips cracked. "I have watched you play," he said, "from the inside of these computers, for a long time now."

"I've never played here," Curtis said. "That's impossible."

The man took a step toward him. "It matters not where you play," he said, tapping his own head. "My mind is inside the machines, inside the cables and wires, inside the Internet. I am inside the realm."

"Um . . . ," Curtis said, "okay. Who are you?"

"Don't you recognize me?" the man asked, taking one step into the room so that his face was better lit.

Then he reached into his back pocket and pulled out a long, slim knife — a dagger.

Curtis gasped. "That knife," he said. "It's the Glowing Blade of Thieves, from *Kingdom of Doom.*"

The man nodded. "Yes," he said. "It certainly is."

Curtis felt like he couldn't breathe. "You're King," he whispered. "The thief!"

– Chapter 5: **Realm of Ghosts** –

"You, Hurricane, have given me the best fight of my career," King said. "Do you accept my challenge?"

Curtis shook his head. "Stop calling me Hurricane," he said. "And I'm not accepting anything until you tell me what this challenge is."

"Isn't it obvious?" King asked. He turned and left the office. Junior and Curtis glanced at each other, and then slowly followed him.

Out in the computer room, everything was different. It was still dark, but now all the tables and chairs had been pushed against the walls, except for two.

In the center of the room, a table was set up. On top of it were two computers, and next to it were two chairs.

"Wow," Curtis said. King stood in the center of the room, next to the table with the computers.

"I brought you here, Hurricane, just for the challenge," King went on.

"You didn't bring us," Junior said. "Troy Macintosh did."

King laughed. "You are a fool, friend. You believed that fake voicemail I left on your phone," King said. "But you did what I wanted you to do."

"Fake?" Junior repeated. He frowned. "I guess I should've known," he muttered.

"Okay, so you tricked us," Curtis said. "Now what about the challenge?"

"It is simply this," King said. "If you defeat me, you and your friend may leave."

"And if you win?" Curtis said.

"Then you will stay here forever," King said, "trapped in the network with me."

Curtis looked at the computers. They were the best gaming computers available: super fast, with tons and tons of memory and the best graphics cards in the world. Hurricane would be even faster and stronger than usual. Of course, so would King.

"What if I refuse your challenge?" he asked.

King chuckled, and said, "Then I leave the door locked, and the windows sealed, and you and your friend can stay here and rot."

"He'll take your challenge," Junior said, stepping forward. "And he'll kick your butt, too. Maybe you aren't aware that this guy is the best gamer around."

"Thanks, Junior," Curtis said out of the corner of his mouth. Junior shrugged.

King placed a hand on the monitor of each of the fancy computers. As he did, both screens hummed and began to glow. Soon a game start-up screen was loading.

Junior elbowed Curtis. "Hey, look," Junior whispered, nodding toward the power cords. Both cords had been cut.

"What game is this, anyway?" Curtis asked, staring at one of the screens.

It was showing a creepy castle in the background, with a ghostly figure holding a dagger. The figure seemed to be coming right at Curtis. "I don't recognize it," Curtis said.

"It's new, a pre-release," King said. He sat down at one computer. "It's called *Realm of Ghosts*."

"Hey, wait a minute," Curtis said, looking at the other computer. "I agreed to use Hurricane to fight King, not some new character in a game I've never played."

"The controls are the same as *Kingdom of Doom*," King said. "You shouldn't have any trouble at all." He gestured for Curtis to sit. "And I've already brought Hurricane and King into the game."

Curtis sat down and looked at the monitor.

Sure enough, his avatar, Hurricane, was loaded into the game world. He stood on a cliff overlooking a vast wasteland.

Across from Curtis, King put on a set of headphones with a small microphone attached. They would use the microphones to communicate in-game. Then King pulled up his hood.

Curtis found the set of headphones on his own table and pulled them on. The game had no music, but the sound effects sounded so real.

A haunting wail, like the sound of hundreds of ghosts, filled his head. On the screen, Hurricane looked around, as if he too heard the creepy soundtrack.

Suddenly King's voice came through his headset.

"Go north," he said. "I am waiting for you at the dueling grounds."

Curtis pulled the little microphone down and said into it, "Okay."

He moved Hurricane through the vast wasteland. The sound of crying ghosts became louder. In the distance, he could see lightning storms and woods on fire. Soon Hurricane reached the edge of the woods. Just inside the shadows of trees, King the thief was waiting.

Curtis noticed that the avatar's face was nearly identical to that of the man across from him at the other computer. He wondered if that was why he had recognized the man when his hood first came down.

King gave him no time to prepare. He simply snapped, "Begin!"

Then they were dueling.

Immediately, King used his famous trick. Before Hurricane could even raise his two-handed sword, the thief was behind him, his dagger drawn. Hurricane was stabbed, losing life points right away.

"Ow!" Curtis cried out. Just as Hurricane was attacked in the game, Curtis felt a sharp stab right in his back.

– Chapter 6: **The Blade of Reckoning** –

"Hey, what is this?" Curtis snapped. He jumped up from the chair, feeling his back. Something was sticky on the back of his shirt. Was it blood?

"Are you okay?" Junior whispered. Curtis didn't respond.

King smiled at him. "I told you," he said. "It's pre-release. A new experience in gaming. And you're one of the first to play. It's a full immersion into the game."

"It hurts!" Curtis replied.

King suddenly stopped smiling. "Of course it does," he said angrily. "It's supposed to hurt. Now sit."

Curtis looked at King, then at Junior. Junior shrugged.

Curtis sat down and tried to focus on the game. Hurricane raised his sword, the Blade of Reckoning, and shoved it down, right at the thief.

Across the table, King sucked in his breath, but smiled. Still, Curtis knew he had landed a good hit.

The thief was fast. Really fast. His dagger was moving faster than Hurricane could fight back.

Curtis jumped and twisted in his seat with every little attack King landed.

For every minor hit King managed, Curtis's huge sword did even more damage to his opponent.

After Curtis's fifth successful attack, King fell from his chair. In the game, the thief was badly wounded.

"Finish him off!" Junior said. He was leaning close over Curtis's shoulder. "This is your chance!"

"Yes," King said as he got up and sat back down. "I am badly wounded. You could defeat me easily now and become the champion yourself."

Hurricane raised the Blade of Reckoning and looked down at the wounded thief. Curtis paused. Should he do it? Should he finish off King the thief? For some reason, he couldn't make himself bring down the blade.

"But you won't finish me, will you?" King said, taunting Curtis. "For if you do, you will be the true champion. From inside the realm, from within the system, I will make it known that Hurricane is really Curtis Switzer."

King spat as he spoke Curtis's real name, like it left a bad taste in his mouth. Curtis shuddered.

"Soon everyone will know you, Curtis," he said. "Everyone will know that you are the one who defeated me, Khyber Kingsley, the thief."

"Wait a second. Khyber Kingsley?" Curtis said. "The champion gamer? The one who went missing? That's you? You're him?"

King looked at Curtis over the tops of their monitors. His dry, cracked lips curled into a smile.

"Not missing anymore," King said. "I'm in the game. Always."

Curtis's hands started to shake. He felt a hand on his shoulder, then Junior's breath on his ear.

His friend whispered, "Don't listen to him, Curtis. You're winning. He's just trying to confuse you, to freak you out, so you won't finish him off."

Curtis looked at his monitor.

King the thief was still on the ground. Hurricane still held the Blade of Reckoning up, ready to strike.

"I can't do it," Curtis whispered. "If I beat him, everyone will know I'm Hurricane. Troy will know, everyone at school . . . even writers for the gaming magazine. I can't handle it."

"Curtis, you have to do it," Junior insisted. "If you let him win, we'll be stuck in the game forever, like he is."

Curtis thought about it. It wouldn't be so bad, really, to be stuck in the game forever.

He loved gaming. Maybe being inside the game with King and Junior would be what he'd always wanted.

"Look out, Curtis!" Junior suddenly shouted. "The dagger!"

Curtis snapped out of his thoughts and saw Khyber's hand. It was already on the Glowing Blade of Thieves. He was about to draw, to attack in real life.

"Do it now!" Junior said.

Curtis didn't wait. With a great battle cry, Hurricane brought down the Blade of Reckoning.

King screamed as the weapon struck him, and Khyber Kingsley flew from his chair. The blast from the attack sent him flying into the open office.

The door slammed behind him.

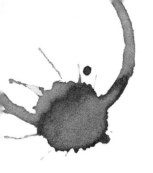

– Chapter 7: **Winner** –

Silence fell over the room. The glow of the two super computers faded quickly.

A voice, calm and gentle, announced, "Winner: Hurricane."

Curtis and Junior looked at the office door. No sounds came from behind it.

A moment later, the lights overhead began to turn on. Around the room, the desks and chairs were no longer against the walls. The computers were dusty.

"Did that really happen?" Junior asked.

"I think so. Unless we imagined it," Curtis said.

"We can't have imagined the exact same thing," Junior said.

Curtis got up from his chair. "Then it really happened," he said. He started walking toward the office door.

"What are you doing?" Junior said. He jumped up to stop Curtis and grabbed his arm.

"I want to see if he's in there, if he's okay," Curtis said. "Besides, the emergency exit is in there, remember?"

Then something caught Junior's eye.

"Look," Junior said. He pointed at the corkboard beside the office door.

There, among flyers for computers for sale, ads for new games, and apartment rentals, was a single newspaper article. It looked hastily torn from a recent issue.

Curtis leaned in close and read the headline out loud. "Gaming champ Khyber Kingsley dies in electrical accident at local gaming club." He looked at the article's date. "This is from a week ago."

"Whoa," Junior whispered. "So who was the guy you dueled against?"

Curtis shrugged. "Maybe Khyber didn't really die in the electrical accident," he said. "Maybe he got sucked into the game. And now that I've defeated him —"

"Now he can rest in peace?" Junior suggested.

"Something like that," Curtis said.

Junior looked around. "Let's get out of here," he said. He shivered. "That's the last time I go to one of Troy's parties."

The boys turned away from the office door and headed to the front of the building. There, the door that had been boarded up stood open, inviting them to leave.

When they left, the door slammed and locked behind them.

Case number: 48948

Date reported: April 14

Crime scene: DigiGame gaming club, Warehouse District, Ravens Pass

Local police: Officer Mary Carlson, with the force for 15 years; Detective John Gregg, with the force 7 years

Civilian witnesses: Curtis Switzer, age 13; Tom "Junior" Yackish, Jr., age 13

Disturbance: During a routine sweep of the area, police noticed lights on and noise coming from the DigiGame club, which had been closed for remodeling. Further inspection found no evidence of people inside. Still, something seemed off, so they called me in.

Suspect information: None.

CASE NOTES:

I WAS CALLED IN AT AROUND 3 IN THE MORNING.
THE OFFICERS HAD LEFT, AND THERE WAS NO SIGN
OF ANYONE NEARBY. I USED SPECIAL EQUIPMENT TO
CHECK THE AREA FOR ELECTROMAGNETIC ACTIVITY.
THEN I FOUND THE VIDEO CAMERAS.

IT'S HARD TO TELL JUST WHAT WENT ON, BECAUSE
THE VIDEO WAS SHAKY AND CUT IN AND OUT. IT
SEEMS THE TWO CIVILIAN WITNESSES HAD ENTERED,
BEEN THREATENED, AND WERE UNABLE TO LEAVE.
AT ONE POINT, ONE OF THE KIDS SITS DOWN AT A
COMPUTER AND PLAYS A GAME. THAT'S WHEN THE
TAPE BLACKS OUT.

IT WASN'T UNTIL I INTERVIEWED THE TWO CIVILIANS
THAT I FOUND OUT WHAT HAD GONE DOWN THAT
NIGHT.

I CONDEMNED THE BUILDING. DIGIGAME WON'T OPEN.

DEAR READER,

THEY ASKED ME TO WRITE ABOUT MYSELF. THE FIRST
THING YOU NEED TO KNOW IS THAT JASON STRANGE IS
NOT MY REAL NAME. IT'S A NAME I'VE TAKEN TO HIDE MY
TRUE IDENTITY AND PROTECT THE PEOPLE I CARE ABOUT.
YOU WOULDN'T BELIEVE THE THINGS I'VE SEEN, WHAT
I'VE WITNESSED. IF PEOPLE KNEW I WAS TELLING THESE
STORIES, SHARING THEM WITH THE WORLD, THEY'D TRY TO
GET ME TO STOP. BUT THESE STORIES NEED TO BE TOLD,
AND I'M THE ONLY ONE WHO CAN TELL THEM.

I CAN'T TELL YOU MANY DETAILS ABOUT MY LIFE. I CAN
TELL YOU I WAS BORN IN A SMALL TOWN AND LIVE IN
ONE STILL. I CAN TELL YOU I WAS A POLICE DETECTIVE
HERE FOR TWENTY-FIVE YEARS BEFORE I RETIRED. I CAN
TELL YOU I'M STILL OUT THERE EVERY DAY AND THAT
CRAZY THINGS ARE STILL HAPPENING.

I'LL LEAVE YOU WITH ONE QUESTION—IS ANY OF THIS
TRUE?

JASON STRANGE
RAVENS PASS

Glossary

abandoned (uh-BAN-duhnd)—deserted, or no longer used

avatar (AV-uh-tar)—a movable icon representing a game's player

challenge (CHAL-uhnj)—an invitation to fight

dagger (DAG-ur)—a short, pointed weapon

duel (DOO-uhl)—a fight between two people

grounds (GROUNDZ)—the land surrounding a large building

immersion (i-MUR-zhuhn)—being completely inside something

inconvenience (in-kuhn-VEE-nyunss)—trouble

opponent (uh-POH-nuhnt)—someone who is against you in a fight

realm (RELM)—kingdom

vast (VAST)—huge

villains (VIL-uhnz)—wicked people

wasteland (WAYST-land)—an area where few plants can live

DISCUSSION QUESTIONS

1. Who was King?

2. What are your favorite video games? What makes a video game fun to play?

3. What was the creepiest part of this book? Explain your answer.

WRITING PROMPTS

1. Create your own video game. Give it a name and draw a picture of the box it comes in. What kinds of things happen in the game? What kinds of characters are in it? Describe everything about your game.

2. Imagine what would have happened if, when the boys got to DigiGame, the party was happening, just like they thought it would. Write a short story that tells what happens.

3. Curtis is secretly amazing at video games. What's your secret talent? Write about it.

Weird
THINGS
Happen in
RAVENS
PASS.

JASON STRANGE

writes about them.

JASON STRANGE

To
Wake the Dead

JASON

Zombie

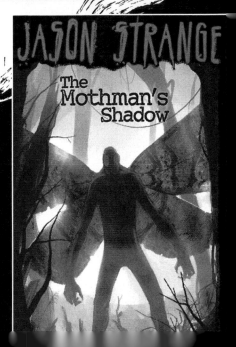

JASON STRANGE

The
Mothman's
Shadow